To Lyn and Earl Abrams, to the memory of my mother,
and, of course, to Harvey and Emma

Library of Congress Catalog Card Number: 93-83611

ISBN 0-590-47003-5

12 11 10 9 8 7 6 5 4 3 2 1   4 5 6 7 8 9 9/10

Printed in Singapore   37

First Scholastic printing, October 1994

Light the Lights!

A Story about Celebrating
HANUKKAH & CHRISTMAS

Written and illustrated by
Margaret Moorman

Cartwheel
·B·O·O·K·S·®
Scholastic Inc.
New York Toronto London Auckland Sydney

It happened the same way every winter, when
the world grew cold and afternoons became dark long
before dinnertime. . . .

One morning, Emma's father raised the shades in her room and said, "Sweetheart! Tonight's the first night of Hanukkah! Time to get out the menorah!"

After breakfast, Emma helped him take
the old silver menorah out of the cabinet
in the dining room. They unwrapped it carefully,
then polished it with soft cloths and pink cream
until it gleamed.

That evening, at sundown, Emma's father
sang the ancient blessing. Her mother steadied
Emma's hand to help her pass the flame from the
shammash candle to the first Hanukkah candle.

Every night for a week and a day, they added another candle. Emma's father would say, "Let's light the lights!" And the ceremony would begin.

The menorah sat on a table by the living room window, where all the people rushing home from work and all the neighbors up and down the street could catch a glimpse of it.

Some nights Emma watched until the candles burned down to their holders.

On the fourth night, Uncle Ken and Aunt Betsy
came to Emma's house with her cousins Sam and Kate.
"There are strange lumps in my coat pockets,"
Uncle Ken complained. Emma and Sam reached in
and pulled out pouches of Hanukkah gelt. Peeling
back the wrappers of the fat gold coins, they found
sweet milk chocolate inside.

Kate was too little to play dreidel, but she
liked to watch Sam and Emma spin the top.
When it was time for dinner, Kate tasted her
first latkes, the crisp potato pancakes made
especially for Hanukkah.

Grandma Rose came to celebrate the eighth night.
She and Emma danced together hand in hand.
"O Hanukkah, O Hanukkah, Come light the
menorah," they sang.

At last all the candles were lighted. The full menorah
looked so beautiful reflected in the dark panes of
the window.

T hen one day, Emma's mother pulled down boxes of Christmas ornaments from the top shelf of the closet.

"Well, Pumpkin, shall we pick out the Christmas tree this morning?" she asked.

Emma put on her jacket, boots, scarf, and mittens and went outside with her parents to search for the perfect tree.

Last year, Emma had picked a short, fat, bushy one. This year she chose a tall one with a branch at the top that was skinny and straight—just right for the ornament Emma liked best, the fragile glass star.

The tree was heavy, so Emma helped her mother and father carry
it home. They all said Merry Christmas to their neighbor Ann. Her
dog Fluffy was wearing a new red jacket.

"He opened his present early," Ann said.

After lunch, Emma's friends Natalia and Patrick came over to help
trim the tree. Emma's mother set out cups of hot chocolate and a tray
of Christmas cookies. There were gingerbread men, sugar cookies shaped
like trees and reindeer, and little white, powdery balls with nuts inside.

Emma's father played the piano, and everyone
sang "Joy to the World." Emma knew the whole
tune and most of the words by heart.

When all of the decorations were out of their boxes and on the tree, Emma's mother said, "Let's light the lights!" Every bough sparkled with silvery tinsel and shiny glass balls.

On Christmas Eve, while Emma was sleeping in the dark house, Santa Claus came quietly and left presents under the tree. He also turned on the lights for Christmas morning. How did he know Emma would wake up before dawn?

After the holidays, Emma helped wrap
the Hanukkah menorah and the Christmas
ornaments and put them away for next year.

But she remembered the bright winter lights
in the dark winter nights for a long, long time.

T
12.95